good deed rain

# 40 Books by Allen Frost

...Ohio Trio...Bowl of Water...
....Another Life....Home Recordings....
...The Mermaid Translation...The Selected
Correspondence of Kenneth Patchen....
...The Wonderful Stupid Man...
..Saint Lemonade...Playground...Roosevelt..
....5 Novels....The Sylvan Moore Show....
...Town in a Cloud....A Flutter of Birds
Passing Through Heaven: A Tribute to Robert
Sund......At the Edge of America......
...Lake Erie Submarine....The Book of Ticks...
........I Can Only Imagine........
....The Orphanage of Abandoned Teenagers....
...Different Planet...Go with the Flow: A
Tribute to Clyde Sanborn...Homeless Sutra...
..The Lake Walker....A Hundred Dreams Ago..
....Almost Animals....The Robotic Age....
....Kennedy....Fable....Elbows & Knees:
Essays & Plays....The Last Paper Stars....
...Walt Amherst is Awake...When You Smile
You Let in Light....Pinocchio in America....
....Florida....Blue Anthem Wailing....
...The Welfare Office...Island Air...
..Imaginary Someone..Violet of the Silent
Movies...The Tin Can Telephone...

# The
# TIN CAN
# TELEPHONE

*The Tin Can Telephone* © 2020
Allen Frost, Good Deed Rain
Bellingham, Washington
ISBN: 9781646335596

Writing and Illustrations: Allen Frost
Cover Production: Jen Armitage
Apple: TFK!

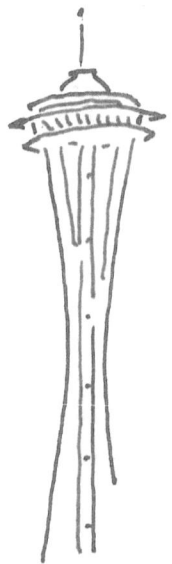

# The TIN CAN TELEPHONE

Allen Frost

Good Deed Rain ◊ Bellingham, Washington ◊ 2020

# CONTENTS

# DIRECTIONS

All this happened a long time ago, in a city that is no longer there. Believe me, I've tried to find it. I've looked for landmarks, laundromats and bowling alleys, I've followed old cement sidewalks until they cracked. I can stand in the same place, but that world is gone. It's amazing how fast Seattle ran over its past. I guess it proves an even older Buddhist lesson on temporality. At least it seems to be, but I wonder...I don't think so. I have reason to believe that past exists in another place.

Quite by accident I found a way to make contact again. I didn't need a mad scientist from *The Count Misfit Show* to create a time machine out of Tesla coils and chemistry. The parts can be found at the grocery store for just a few dollars. You probably already have what you need at home, it's easy to make. When I made that discovery, the past came back to me as if it never went away. Although I grew older and the memories grew further and further away from me, now we're connected by string.

When I was a boy, I listened to a lot of 1940s programs on my transistor radio. I loved the way sound alone could create a whole living visible world. This illusion was so true I actually felt like I was with Jack Benny on some sunny California day, or following Boston Blackie below the pier on the waterfront at night. That wonder never left. So I don't think it's impossible to listen in on the past. It's always there in the airwaves; you just need the right kind of radio, or something even simpler. A Tin Can Telephone will do. The directions are easy enough:

1) You will need 2 empty tin cans and a roll of string.

2) With a hammer and nail, punch a hole (just big enough for the string to go through) in the bottom of each can.

3) Push the string up through the hole and tie a knot so it can't slip back through the bottom of the can.

4) Hold the open end of the can to your ear and have a friend talk into theirs. The string will carry the sound to you.

# TIN CAN SIGNALS

I remember the first time I made one of those when I was young, pulling the string taut across the room, and the voice of Jesse or Olsen coming through. I didn't know how it worked, but it did. It was a sort of magic I just believed in. And when I discovered it still works, I was surprised all over again.

The sound is broadcasting from those childhood days. Just like Jack Benny entering the vault under his Beverly Hills mansion, I am projected. I hear something. When I close my eyes I am in another world.

I see a vacant lot I remember. We used to press through the gap in the chain link fence, and follow the trail we trampled into tall weeds. I convinced everyone the pile of gravel in the middle of the yard is Mount Fuji. It has been shrunk into a 10 foot mountain and shipped here in a crate. I warn them we better run, "Quick! You never know if it's going to erupt back to its normal size!" We climb the wooden fence, one by one. As usual Billy Mitchell pushes ahead and is the first one over. When he hits the ground he holds his hand pinned between his knees, afraid to look. He got a splinter crawling off the top. Olsen drops down beside me. Billy keeps his hand balled up as he runs across the lawn in the direction of his house. When he jumps the curb he yelps something back to us. He is gone. This is just like one of those Tarzan movies on TV. Someone always falls prey to an alligator or a jaguar, or a poison tipped arrow. We can't let that stop us, we have to keep going. We still have a long way back to the tree.

The vacant lot isn't the only place I find myself. The tin can signals come from many sources. There's a jukebox full of them. Each one has a song of its own that plays in the tin can telephone. Sometimes it's the P-Patch, an overgrown jungle I pretend is Africa as I follow the path across to the next sidewalk. Sometimes I'm on a playground that turns into an ocean with a pirate ship. Once after raining all week, a wide shallow pool forms behind Kristine's house. I want there to be fish in it. Barracudas and swordfish. We lay boards across the corner so we can watch them swim. Another day I play in a big plot of fresh earth where they are starting to build a house. We hop rebar and climb cement. King Kong lives in a burrowed cave below.

Destinations could be just about anywhere momentary. I could tell they were fragile and rare. My Tin Can Telephone is drawn to those places.

On a day like this when I had nothing else to do, I listened for the next signal.

At first all I could hear was what you would expect from a metal soup can.

Then it feels real as a fairytale, the sound of leaves, sunlit breeze in the heights of a magic bean stalk. It's still there, I am picturing it now and it exists.

From the top of the tree, I can see all of Seattle, the buildings and clouds and Olympic Mountains to the west and on a clear day Mount Rainier. Closer by, I see the church tower spire and our green house and my bedroom window below the eaves. This is how the birds feel, this is why they sing. Sometimes I pretend to be a bird and I can open my wings and go wherever I want. The city is still filled in with forest, with all the toy houses tucked about, slanted roofs and TV aerials, chimneys and telephone wires, like a railroad set you'd find in a museum display, a world so real you wish you could fit inside there and explore. My favorite game up here is Swiss Family Robinson. We just saw that movie and this tree in my neighbor's yard makes that movie real. The way up, each branch and edge in the trunk is a stairway that goes to rooms stacked in the leaves. I sit up there in the tower and listen to the neighborhood. Other kids playing, a dog barking, a radio, a crow, a car on Woodlawn Avenue, my name called from the ground.

# DIRT GARDEN

There was a song on the radio a lot at that time. I hear the radio on the window sill playing "Seasons in the Sun" while I climb our fence to the gate, unlatch it and jump to the ground. The dandelions grow between our houses. The blue push mower will reappear and they'll be gone but they'll be back again. I know the neighbor's backyard the way I know ours and I run underneath the clothesline on the way to the dark pool of shadow below the climbing tree. I surprise two yellow butterflies from their flowers. The tomatoes are staked with sticks and string. The tiger-tail swing hangs off a branch on a long yellow rope. Usually I start climbing right away. That first step up the trunk is polished from my sneaker tread. I know the next branch to grab and where my next footstep will go. Not this time though.

I have to check on Dirt Garden. It's dirt alright, but not really a garden. It's a whole town. I guess I should call it Dirt Town, but that doesn't sound right and anyway it's too late. It's already named. Olsen and I have been working on it for a while. We gather branches under the climbing tree, or withered stalks snapped off smaller plants. Bundling up as many as we can from around the yard, we carry them to the trampled ground where Olsen's backyard begins. These will be the walls and roofs of little buildings and become bridges, fences and towers. Making houses is fun, laying the sticks over each other like Lincoln Logs. The wind and rain make sure we have a lot of repairs to do. Sometimes a cat will leave footprints through it. A temporary guest. We also catch bugs and bring them to live in this town, as if this is the dream they have always been wanting. One day a giant hand will appear from the sky and find me too. I don't know if the bugs took to living there. They do what they want to do. They probably prefer being in the weeds and holding on to leaves.

Olsen is already in his backyard. The scarecrow sunlight, the sound of a loud seaplane overhead. I can't tell what he's looking at, maybe a spider web. I don't think I have ever called him on the phone. We just show up in the same place at the same time. "Look!" he says.

There's something in the garden. I'll have to be closer before I can tell what it is. I hope it's one of those Roly Poly bugs. They remind me of the gray VW Beetle Olsen's family has. When they moved to Oregon in that I would never see him again.

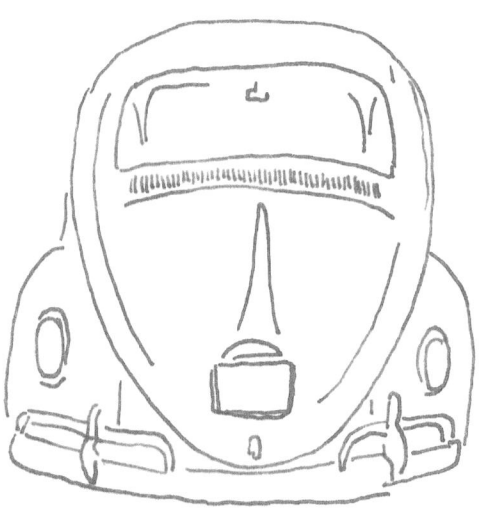

# OVERNIGHT at OLSEN'S

Olsen's house is sweet with incense. The same smell as those shops on the Ave, with lava lamps and jewelry in the window, statues from India with the arms everywhere, strange music crowding the door. Heavy pillow chairs are dropped on Olsen's living room floor. The theme for *Bonanza* plays in the big wooden console color TV. Every house I visit has a different television, with different channels on. Black and white or bright as crayons, mysteries and comedies, foreign movies, or the shows I would watch with my grandparents on their bed, like *Perry Mason*, with a cigarette going next to me.

You have to part the strings of beads to get into Olsen's kitchen. A newspaper photo of Gloria sticks on the refrigerator. I know her from *All in the Family* but maybe she means something more. Olsen gets the milk out of there and we pour bowls of cereal. The poster near the sink reads: *A Woman's Place is in the White House*. It's ten o'clock and we still have a while before Count Misfit starts—an hour of cowboys and commercials to go. His mom and dad are upstairs, you can hear their record playing, and a red candle is going, set on the bannister. They stay up there—we're on our own here. The loud commercial for a used car lot is telling us we'd be crazy not to buy, but we're looking for spoons in the silverware drawer. Olsen holds up a single chopstick. We always find something to laugh about. We bring our bowls back to the living room and Olsen does a funny walk and I spill some milk onto my sock. The tapestry of a skull thinking of a lightning bolt watches us from the wall with hollowed narrow eyes. Tonight's movie is *The Monolith Monsters*. I saw the commercial for it last night. I told Olsen at school and he invited me to watch it on his color TV. I said I didn't know if it was in black and white or color. Our television is black and white and that's the way everything looks. It will take years before I realize *The Wizard of Oz* turns into color. A blazing American Wild West fills the screen as we sit. I like the chairs in his house. You feel like you're on a beanbag cloud. One hour to wait. If we can survive all these cowboys and not fall asleep, Count Misfit will appear.

all she needed to say

# BASEBALL

I like to listen to baseball on the car radio when I drive Interstate 5. It's two hours from where we live now, back to Seattle…Edison, Burlington, La Conner, Mount Vernon, Arlington, Marysville, Everett, and further south. The AM signal crackles and slips in and out of music. Sometimes late at night, you can catch a strong transmission from California, hear the Angels or the Oakland A's.

The light shines under my bedroom door like a long white candle lying down. While trying to sleep, I imagine myself as a baseball hero, with my own baseball card and gum that doesn't taste like cardboard. I'm also married to Delynne. That's hard to imagine though. Will she always have that cold, with a runny nose? Standing there by home plate, I look across at the stands and there she is, waving a handkerchief at me. We have two daughters and two sons and they're all waving smaller handkerchiefs. They look like a surrendering family. That was about as far as I went with that thought. I know I won't be a baseball player. I'm not even in the Little League. I went to tryouts at the Green Lake Field, but it didn't go well. The coach reminded me of a World War Two movie, one of those black and white sergeants yelling at his men. I was hoping for Walter Matthau and the Bad News Bears, but it was nothing like that. So baseball is out.

But I did go to Delynne's house. I went with her on a school bus to the other side of town.

We get out on the corner and walk to a little house. Her mother is already home and she invites us into the kitchen. Delynne asks her for Twinkies. I have to admit that's how she got me here. At school lunch she was eating one and she told me, "You can come to my house. We have Twinkies all the time." That's all she needed to say. I recognize one of her crayon drawings taped on the refrigerator. The wall clock is interesting, it's shaped like Felix the Cat and his eyes move back and forth with his waving tail. He seems happy enough. Her mother gets two Twinkies from a box on the counter and passes me one. A crackly cellophane surrounds it. Delynne tears hers open with her teeth. "Come on," she says, "I'll show you my room." She leaves her wrapper on the table and I do too. The hallway is painted the same colors as the clothes she wears, as if walking along here in the morning dresses her. I wonder if maybe that's because the house is her real mother and she was born in the room we're going to. The rooms of girls are interesting. The colors are different and so are the things they put on their shelves. I don't know, some of it's okay. My neighbor Kathy has a set of Disneyland books. Anytime I'm in her room I sit down on that blue carpet and read them. Delynne's room looks like something the tide washed aside. It's all a bit windblown. Her blankets are splashed around and half on the floor. She must throw herself out every morning. And then of all things, she points me to a pink plastic toy house. A purple car is overturned beside it and a Barbie doll has fallen out. Oh no—I already know—that's what she wants to play with.

# FLYING

Glenn Miller's doomed big band starts every school morning with "In the Mood." I have a bowl of cereal or French toast, oatmeal if I'm not so lucky. That familiar song always makes me think of J.P. Patches' show, as if he gathered all the notes among the things people threw away and stuck them together to play. I never once doubted that a clown lives in our city dump. He is part of our daily reality. He has his shack out there and like a dignitary he greets boys and girls lucky enough to find their way there. If we can't be there, he will find us with his ICU2TV, looking right into our room.

I've been waiting for him to spin that twirling target shaped wheel on his door. That makes an old cartoon appear, or Flash Gordon, or what I'm waiting for this morning—Rocket Man's next installment—*Chapter 10: The Deadly Fog*. With a roar he flies right out of the gray sky into the back of the truck carrying the Decimator. How lucky can you get? He got out just in time before it blew up. I wish I had that rocket suit he wears. I've even been practicing, pretending I have the selector on my coat that will make me take off. I run along the sidewalk and with a jump I spring into the air. Next thing you know, the rocket motor roars as it takes me over the roofs and trees. I hold my hands in front of me, streamlined, and I can see the other kids heading off to school. They look up from the ground and wave. The ten blocks I walk every day go by so fast underneath, I have to swoop back around to find a good spot on the playground. I turn the dial on my suit to *Slow* and *Land* and there I am touching down by the Monkey Bars. There's always someone hanging on to those iron rings and I know the feeling, I've spent a lot of time wishing that was really flying too.

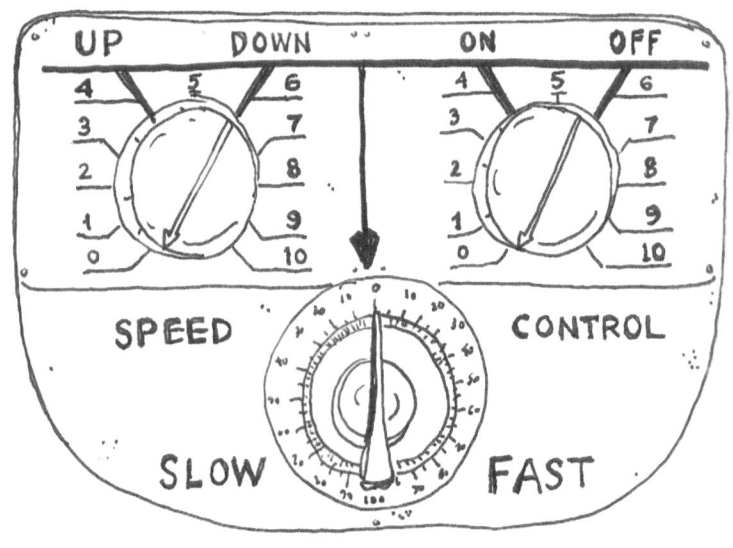

following the dial

"You don't know where we are!" Ty tells us angrily. When he gets mad his face blotches red and if he's close enough to grab you, you're in trouble. You don't want to be crushed in those arms. He seizes the compass from Jesse. "Give me the map too!" It's not really a map, it's just a list of coordinates. We are supposed to follow it and find somewhere at the end—who knows what. When you're a Cub Scout you follow orders. I guess it's not that different than the Army. "You dummies can find your own way!"

Jesse and I watch him leave. His blue untucked shirt, his boots stomping branches, we let him go. I know this park already. I only live down this hill a ways. When Jesse comes over, sometimes we walk here and play *Time Tunnel*, running from dinosaurs, finding ourselves in a future world where the Morlocks come out of the ground at dusk. Following the dial on that crazy compass has led us into the brush.

"It's okay," I say. Jesse's my friend and we're not going to get lost on this foreign planet. I check the sky for pterodactyls before I push a leafy branch aside.

Our scout leader Mr. Toms divided everyone up into groups of three and scattered us around Woodland Park. He's probably waiting for us at a picnic table somewhere.

"Careful, there might be quicksand," I warn Jesse. I pick up a stick and prod the ground. "I think we're okay."

Off in the distance we hear a kid yell. It might be Ty getting chewed by a saber tooth tiger.

"Should we go that way?" Jesse says.

"No. That sounds like a trap."

Jesse nods. He would follow me anywhere.

It seems like we should be going back towards the parking lot. Our parents will be waiting to pick us up pretty soon. We made a lot of wrong twists and turns with that plastic compass, but I think we're just a few hills away. The big trees stand around us like in Red Riding Hood. I take a quick look at each one we pass to figure the fastest way to climb if a wolf shows up.

There's something else besides the sound of our shoes in the leaves. I hear it and Jesse hears it too. Strange voices carry through the woods.

If I had to guess, I would say there's a cartoon

beyond the next ridge.

"I wonder if that's where we're supposed to end up."

Jesse might be right. I agree, "Let's take a look."

A dog is barking, but it sounds more like a person pretending to be one.

Climbing the last crumbling slant of hill, grabbing hold of roots, our shoes and pockets filling with soil, we leave a little landslide of dirt and stones skittering behind us.

A loud sound like thunder and a quacking duck.

As we crawl onto the weedy top of the cliff, we have a good view of the scene below.

A crowd of kids and families sit on the grass surrounding an old truck. Charlie Chaplin could have parked it on the lawn and set the stage. Actors dressed as a rocket crew all pull on a long rope leash looped around someone in a dog suit. The rope wraps him and continues taut from him and ends in the hands of five green painted Martians. The dog staggers back and forth between the two groups. We've played tug-of-war at school but not with a dog tied in the middle. Seems mean. A Lizardman wearing a bib is holding a plate, drumming on it with a fork. It's obvious he's waiting to eat the poor dog. Everyone is cheering for the dog who is really hamming it up. A girl in the front row is urgently telling him what to do.

Jesse reads the banner that's planted in the ground beside the truck, "Rocky Jones and the Space Polka Patrol."

And then another thunder crash and stepping from a cardboard box labeled Teleporter, smoke pouring around him, Flash Gordon appears! I recognize the sun on his uniform, it's the same one he wears in those old black and white serials. He looks like he's been wearing it for 50 years.

In the confusion, I laugh as the dog squirms free of the rope, leaving it to the two tug-of-war teams. With a big shrug, he lies underneath the line and reads a newspaper.

Who needs a compass and paperwork to drag us somewhere else? It was better to be lost and see where being lost would take us.

where being lost would take us

# DRIVING

A Volkswagen motor underneath the seat is a sound I got used to after going across country so many times. Leaving Washington, across Idaho, staring out the window at Montana where it really feels true the hills are watching you too. The hot wind stuck in the side window roars. Another sound I also got used to, our dog panting over the backseat, staring straight ahead. Only a blink ago we would have been in prairie schooners and she would have been running beside us. Old Mr. Larson in the house across the street told me about coming to Seattle in a covered wagon. I think of him, going so much slower, rocking back and forth, and the creak of wooden wheels. Horses turned into cars in his lifetime.

# A CALL to PRAYER

An echo of nightmarish screams and Halloween sound effects fill the nighttime air. We have passed the bright stalls with darts and balloons and bowling pins, and loud shooting galleries, bells and buzzing and crowds, the roller coaster roar, the Flight to Mars, and we cross the grassy black hills around the Fun Forest. Below us now, we have a good view of the KJR Haunted House.

This is the only time I will see Count Misfit in person, from a distance, in a green spotlight on stage with J.P. Patches next to him. Their voices are a murmur lost in everyone's shadows. I wasn't ready for this to sound so scary. Ghosts are moaning, chains are dragging, a wolf is howling at the tall flower of the Space Needle. I'm trying my best to be brave as Flash Gordon, but this is quite a test.

Jesse doesn't seem to mind though. He's a couple steps ahead of me. He turns around when he realizes I have frozen and waves our red tickets in his hand. "Come on!"

The haunted house begins on the other side of the stage. A giant spider with flaming eyes clings to a chain link enclosure. It looks like the creature from *The Angry Red Planet* and I don't like the thought of joining the line next to it. Only imagining Buster Crabbe beside me got me there. The screaming gets louder, the witch's cackle, the voodoo drum beat. Jesse gives me my ticket and I hold it tight. We get behind some laughing teenagers and we are moving again. Jesse says something I can't hear, but I force a smile.

We get as close as the ticket taker, a monster who holds out a bandaged hand. Jesse gives him a ticket. I'm next but I have already seen beyond, realizing what is waiting for us just past the spider's web. The bunched line narrows to single file and is forced to pass an iron cage. It barely contains a gorilla. A girl screeches and jumps just out of its reach. The bars aren't able to stop it from clawing out its furry arms and hands. It stomps and beats the cage, waiting for Jesse.

"Come on!" someone behind me gives me a shove.

Of course I have seen hundreds of gorillas before on *The Count Misfit Show* and the Sunday afternoon *Jungle Theatre* and I know how fierce they can be. I'm not taking any chances with this precious life. I turn around and run back up the hill. If Jesse survives, I'll watch for him from where it's safe to thank my lucky stars.

another illusion

# PROJECTIONS

A film projector clacks like Rumpelstiltskin making gold in a dark castle room. Anytime we see a film in class, we beg, "Please! Please!" to watch it backwards when it's done. The teacher holds up her hands to quiet us down. With all the window shades drawn, the room is coppery, our shiny desktops reflect. A bright white square of light projects on the screen pulled over the blackboard. There is so much ceremony to wheeling that machine in, attaching and stringing the reels, uncoiling the electric cord to the socket in the wall, dimming the day and moving the desks to the right and left to make room for the beam of light.

The teacher has another illusion too. When she uses the overhead projector to show evolution or maps, sometimes she will put up a transparency of the American flag. She tells us to stare hard at the red, white and blue. "Keep looking at it for a minute, don't look away, starting…Now!" And we all stare fiercely. Don't blink that will ruin it! The projector hums. Everyone is quiet and then the minute is over and she turns the machine off and still staring at the same spot on the now black screen, we see a green striped flag and everyone marvels, "Cool!" while she explains how the human eye works and why we are seeing something different than before.

But the highlight of her class is the prize she gives every month. Each time it's something different—a balsa wood airplane, a kaleidoscope flashlight, and one time it was a gyroscope! The look on the girl's face who won that—"Amy, can I try it?" She placed it on her desk for all to see. Another time it was a red and white pump rocket you fill with water and fire at the sky—I wanted that so badly I waited until summer and asked for one for my birthday. But even when I got it that August, I didn't have it for long. My grandfather insists he try it out first, and I hand it over to him and we all follow outside to the backyard, tall pine trees all around. I am leaping about excited, "Fire it! Fire it!" And he does. A *fsssssh!* noise as he holds it at arm's length and it's gone. Up so high into the sky we all lost track of where it went. Doubting if it ever came down, we search, but we never find it again. It might have landed in Amelia Earhart's pocket.

The teacher keeps the next prize on the top

left corner of the chalkboard, behind her desk where we worship it with hopeful eyes, prayers, immense longing, and then groaning when someone else wins it. This routine occupies our days in her class. There she will be, teaching in front of us, reading *Blackjack*, the story of an alligator, and we will all be watching that prize pinned up there, casting spells at it to be the lucky one.

# The LOST DOG

Our yard is elevated above the sidewalk, held from spilling onto the street by a cement wall about five feet tall. That means our house and our neighbors' on either side are on a hill like castles. The wall would be good protection if the block ever flooded and we had to row to get anywhere. This wall is also a perfect chalkboard for scratching drawings. I prefer monsters breathing out lightning, or a giant octopus pulling down a ship. Once I wrote FREE LEMONADE, but I had to change it slightly after people started to ask. Nobody wanted it when it became FEET LEMONADE. As ferocious as my pictures may be, my sister and the neighbor girls are sure to surround what I've done with flowers, smiling bumblebees, names in hearts, and horses, always horses. All they ever want to play is horses. What kind of game is that? Running around the yard skittishly and neighing. A horse can't climb the tree or hold out arms to become an airplane on Pacific duty. Horses can't read either, but those girls have plenty of horse books on their shelves: *Black Beauty, Blaze and the Gypsies, Misty of*

*Chincoteague, Stormy: Misty's Foal, Brighty of the Grand Canyon.*

A dog barks on the sidewalk behind me. I never saw it before, a black puppy with white markings. Nobody is with it, it just found me. We already have a dog, she's inside, but she can't come out on the sidewalk without a leash—if she did she would bolt for the distant sound of the zoo up on Phinney Ridge. She's done that before.

"Who are you?" I ask. I stop adding teeth to the dinosaur's mouth and set the chalk down.

The puppy has no collar. It's so friendly it jumps up in my arms. Its tongue is all over my neck and ear. Holding it is like grasping a watery thing. We're not allowed to keep it though, one dog is enough. It doesn't matter if I press its face up to mine. We try to keep it from jumping out of the wagon as we go around the block, knocking on any door we think it might have come from.

# DREAM MUSEUM

*Clang!* I love to pull the rope at the end of the wooden trolley. This brass bell used to warn those people you see in old silent movies. I run my hand along the waxed handrail. I can't believe people used to travel through the city this way. It's like being in a dream at this museum. Diorama displays of sailing ships and towns with rivers and locks, tiny paths to and fro. I can imagine myself in there. I pretend the trolley is moving when I jump off at the next room. An entire seaplane you can almost hear and a hydroplane you can still feel the cold water spray. A periscope goes up through the roof and lets you see the parking lot. If there are any ships to sink, you need to find them in the crosshairs. If you twist it the right way you can see the anti-aircraft gun among the cars. We always run to it when we're done and sit in that metal chair. We target airplanes above Seattle, then we hop off into Montlake Park with its bark trail and bridges and paths. Canoes under the freeway off-ramps. Take your eye from the periscope and you're back inside. The slanted blue carpet leads past a B-47 canopy. We go through rooms that become time capsules with life-size dolls stuck where they were. Downstairs by the water fountain, Bobo the gorilla is embalmed in a glass case. I have a feeling he could still be alive. Look at those eyes. Quick, let's get away! I spend a lot of the time running, I have to see as much as I can, knowing I might wake up any second and it will all be gone.

Perry Como comes on the radio singing "The Bluest Skies You've Ever Seen Are in Seattle" and it's raining so hard you can hear every single ping on the roof of our Volkswagen van. I understand the joke and the irony but I can't help singing along. When you're a kid in the back of a car, you listen and the world slides by.

I watch the buildings and trees and passing cars. The road to Jesse's house takes a while, longer than one song. Raining doesn't seem to mind, it only pulls us along in its stream. There are other songs I know, "Band on the Run" and "Delta Dawn." I wait for "Seasons in the Sun."

I know that driveway we finally pull into beside his car.

"Okay," I say, "We'll be right back."

I open the loud sliding door and hop out.

That rain tingles my neck and hands. It's familiar as a ghost we all put up with.

I knock on Jesse's door and wait, knowing he will be the one to open it.

He does.

"Hi."

"Hi."

I follow him inside, knowing this room too, and not surprised the TV is on with *The Flintstones* in the middle of something. Jesse's short dog runs out to greet me and shuffles away once it knows it's me. I like the colors of this cartoon and the way it's drawn but the story seems like it's just a lot of yelling. Jesse gets his shoes on and his mom helps him with a raincoat. Pretty soon we're back in the weather and getting in the van.

We talk about whatever we always talk about and gasoline drives us to where we park.

The Northgate Mall Theater is exactly what you hope it would be. The smell of popcorn, a bustle of other excited kids we're in here with, blue and green posters on the walls, *20,000 Leagues Under the Sea*—that's the one we're going to see. Look at that submarine! I like the way my feet sink just a little bit into the carpet.

When we find our seats, we're only two of who knows how many others also waiting for the movie to play. Soon the lights will dim as the heavy curtains part and a stream of light will flow above our heads. There's nothing like that feeling. I could pass Jesse a spark and he could throw it at the screen for everyone to see.

what is the sound

## An ORDINARY SONG

What is the sound of a mime? A laughing crowd. It takes ten or twenty people to stand around and then a mime can appear. The same thing happens on the Ave when the Hari Krishnas arrive and suddenly you're surrounded by bells and chanting. Anytime we go to the Science Center, chances are good we'll see a mime. Seems like there is always one of them near the International Fountain. I don't know if they step from a door in a tree, already dressed in black and white stripes, hands and face painted ghostly pale. They don't seem to be quite human. I think they really do come from another world, pulling on invisible ropes and pushing at walls nobody else can see. When they look at us, they can't help but try us out, as if each one of us is a different set of clothes. It makes me a little nervous to stop and watch. Other people laugh and clap when a mime steps behind a man with a limp, follows an old woman and her dog, tracks someone holding an umbrella. I don't want to be noticed that way. I'm afraid the minute we turn away, the mime will latch onto me. How will I get rid of him? What if he decides to stay? Walking everywhere I go, doing everything I do, taking over my shadow and sleeping in my room like a bat. I try to avoid eye contact. I look through the trees and watch the red, blue, yellow gondolas creak and rock by high on the wires overhead. When we finally leave, I try to look as nondescript as I can, like an ordinary song you would hear on the radio.

# Or a DINOSAUR EGG

"The Wabash Cannonball" sung in class, the teacher strumming his guitar, all the kids gathered around, singing, clapping with the happy train riding song. We might have been out on a forest trail when I found it, a big round rock, dented and gray, the size of a bowling ball and I named it for the song. It must have been half buried in a creek bed, but I pull it free and I know I have to bring it home. Maybe I could even bring it in to school. It's a long walk back to the car, shoving it and rolling it along the path. I almost give up and let my imagination turn it into a dinosaur egg instead. We couldn't bring that home. I've seen *Reptilicus* and I know what a dinosaur loose in a city can do.

When we park back in front of our house, my father gets the stone out the door, onto the sidewalk. I have to move it step by step, up the cement waterfall. Like some sort of Erie Canal, I push it on the winding concrete walkway until it finds its resting place under the prickling green juniper near the porch where it sat for years, watching like a heavy eye what came and what went.

# HEIDI

Crime crept into our neighborhood—three solemn people are stapling posters to the telephone poles: *"Where is Heidi?"* the kidnapped girl with her smiling face. She is my age, but I don't know her, she went to another school nearby. She looks like Sally, with her long dark hair, happiness and white dress. Gone, and imagining what her parents are going through—and our parents having to tell us what it meant when a kid went missing. We have to walk to school in groups and keep an eye on each other. The Heidi posters look up and down the block on every telephone pole. No more putting your ear against them to listen to that electricity hum through the wood, the telephone poles are to be feared like the book cover of *The Three Robbers*.

The Heidi posters appear at the same time my sister's bicycle is stolen. She left it at the foot of our steps like we always did while she went inside. When she returned, it was gone. Crying for her pink bicycle with the silver sparkle banana seat, stickers and handles flowing with tinsel.

Then those kids who live in the tall white crooked house across the street, something got into them too. They snuck around the wheels of our neighbor's parked car, got low and let the air out, an angry cluster boasting and pushing, wanting to fight not make friends.

The Heidi posters stayed up for weeks and we never heard what happened to her. The newspaper and radio moved on. There was rain and wind. The paper ripped and the torn edges rattle like wings until they raise the whole neighborhood up into the air like pigeons taking off.

# A HOUSE in the RAIN FOREST

We drive two cars, a camping caravan with our next door neighbors. The Olympic National Rain Forest surrounds us with green. The sky disappears, everywhere is trees and moss on everything and ferns as big as bonfires.

Once the tents are tied through the clouds of moss, we run off into the woods, floating inside of them. Kid voices calling, singing like birds. No sounds of cars or cities, just the forest, a damp, living smell cleaner than a laundromat.

We climb over logs, bounce across the spongy ground, the girls turning into horses but it's okay. I stop beside a tree that has windows. A two hundred foot cedar tree, a thousand years old, I put my hands on it. The trunk goes ten feet around to a doorway. "Hey!" I call, "Come look at this!"

The horses arrive stomping and crackling branches and become girls again. I step inside the hollow room and they follow. We stand on a bed of orange wood chips. The walls go up and up, lit now and then by the many windows. It's also a perfect chimney.

We go back out and gather brush and strips

of bark. Two of the girls are finding fish that look like leaves, and berries that might be good. My neighbor holds my hand after we pretend to start the fire. One time we played we were married and I wonder if it's true.

full of wonders

# The RENAISSANCE TV

Guitar strings are plucked carefully and slow as "Tom Dooley" can be played. Honestly, my favorite part of coming to this house for lessons is waiting for the girl before me to be done. I sit alone in the living room and lay my guitar case onto the sea of red shag carpet and watch the Renaissance TV. That's a time we talked about in class, when suddenly artists were appreciated and urged to create cities full of wonders. This TV has been carved from a shining block of wood with spires and columns and dials like diamonds. Every house has a different television but this one is the most fantastic of all. The colors are hypnotizing, made from precious jewels. I'm glad to come here every week, but it would be better by far if I could just sit on this blue cushion sofa and keep watching *That Girl* on TV.

## The BLUE CURTAIN

It's bedlam. I could be in Noah's ark or a cage at the Woodland Park Zoo. But I'm not. I'm at the movies again. *Escape to Witch Mountain* hasn't started yet and every kid in the place is on their feet, yelling and waving at the stage. Up there in front of the pulled blue curtain is a real life movie hero, only this time he brought a silver robot with him. It swivels and clacks one of its pincer hands. "See Buster Crabbe, in Person!" *The Seattle Times* told us. He is visiting Seattle, probably from outer space. Straight from the planet Mongo, Flash Gordon is here! He says something into the microphone but it isn't working, holding it like a broken ray gun. The Merciless Ming is trying to jinx him again but Flash isn't worried, we are all cheering for him. Then, when his robot companion holds out the paper grocery bag he is gripping in one of his steely claws, Flash reaches inside and pulls out a handful of candy. Some of it falls to the stage as he reaches his arm back. That's when the crowd sounds like a rocket ship roar. I've seen him wrestle a space gorilla and toss evil henchmen about with ease, so it doesn't surprise me when some of the taffies fly our way. Jesse and I scramble under the seats and we've got five. Around us more are landing like meteors. We finally come up again with more candy in our hands and the stage is clear, they are gone, the lights are dimming and the blue curtains begin to slowly wave apart with the movie starting.

# The CREATURE

Aquariums and zoos have their own atmosphere, planets within a planet. Even with my eyes closed I know right away where I am—at an aquarium—I know it by the temperature on my skin, the submarine hum that might be power from the moon, as unseen forces hold back an ocean. Sometimes it feels like I'm beneath the city in the tunnels of an underground sea. Windows carved in the walls show off the fish who live in this hidden water. I wonder, next time I'm on the corner by our house: if I tie a hook to a string and lower it into a street grate, will I catch a manta ray?

Moving along with other people from window to window, it's almost like swimming in the air beside the fish. What is air, what is water?

The voices of the crowd echo from corners ahead of me and behind. The light in here is cupped like a candle in cold hands.

An unmarked door is left partially open. I know what happens when you see this in a movie. There will be a lab back there and Frankenstein will be making a new kind of shark that will rise and lurch around my block tonight looking for me.

Nobody notices me leave the carpeted hallway. The room is filled with holding tanks on shelves and sprouting like chimneys from the floor. Bubbling and seaweed swinging in the current. There's a big cement tank beside me. I can't see what's inside it. I try hopping but the rim is a foot above my eye level so I put my hands on the rough edge and pull myself up.

Something cold and clammy brushes at my fingers while I'm dragging myself up to rest on my elbows.

I am looking straight into the eyes of the Creature from the Black Lagoon. That's what I think at first. It has been captured again and chained in this tank until the Army can haul it away. Then it raises an arm lazily from the pool. I stay holding the ledge long enough to see the rows of suckers pinned like wet buttons to its arm, realizing there are seven more arms under the water too, before I drop.

If I was pulled in, all the attendant would find the next morning is my blue tennis shoe floating in the murk of octopus water like the remains of a fateful shipwreck.

painted with bats and lightning

## SON of COUNT MISFIT

Halloween night, I can hear the shrieks rising far up 48th Street from the direction of our house. I see a ghost and a ballerina scatter from the corner. Lights are on in windows and long shadows spill from trick-or-treaters. Last year I was a robot, made from ice cream tubs we got at 31 Flavors. This year I'm Robin Hood and nimble enough to run. I've already gone round the neighborhood enough times to fill my Food Giant bag. A four foot SuperSonic points behind himself and tells me, "Count Misfit's in that house!" as his sister rabbit grins all chocolaty and admits, "I wasn't scared." He says, "You were too!" She holds half a Nestle Crunch as proof, "He gave me this."

I know what's going on though. My dad made a cardboard coffin big enough for him to lie down in. It is painted with bats and lightning bolts. He worked on it all last night. Now it sits on our porch, across from the door. Hiding inside, he listens for the trick-or-treaters coming up the stairs, opening the screen door. He waits for the knock or doorbell. Then suddenly he throws the cardboard lid aside with a Count

Misfit bellow. I hear the screams again as I cross Woodlawn. The porchlight is on, the Count's silhouette stands up there holding out his cape.

# WHEN I was an ASTRONAUT

"Would you like to enter the contest?" the Food Giant checker asks. She passes me a white coloring book page crowded with the animals from the new *Robin Hood* cartoon. The grocery store goes silent, drops away, all my attention is on this drawing. As I look at it, I can already see the crayon colors I will use to fill it up and make it glow like a stain glass window. Along the wall are a hundred other entries from other kids. Some are good. Some of them you can tell are done by babies. Thick pen lines radiate like radio waves. They would sound like someone leaning on a piano. I think my chances are good and I find out the next week when the telephone rings. I hear my mother's voice from the other room say, "Yes, he's here. Can I ask who's calling?" Fifteen minutes later I am there at Food Giant shaking hands with the manager. I remember the Moon landing, the loud cheering parade, the confetti thick as a waterfall. I guess this is how the astronauts felt.

# The PILGRIMAGE

The monorail hums over Seattle downtown streets. The gears underneath the aisle are eggbeater whirs that keep us aloft. I like to stand at the window and feel the height, to watch the cars and yellow taxis glide below. This space-age ride doesn't have far to go from the Fun Forest to the next station. The silver chrome of it slides across the glass storefronts where we get out. An outdoor escalator takes us down to the street. As usual it's a cold rainy winter afternoon and I tuck my hands deep into my jacket.

The department stores, Nordstrom, Frederick & Nelson, Bon Marché, have filled their big windows with mechanical toys and trains and Boeing airplanes flying on wires, cotton snow piles, lights and moving animals. We linger and stare at the changes, but this is only part of the pilgrimage. We don't go in those shiny stores.

We follow the sidewalk in the weather, a lot of wet rained on cement, cold spilled puddles, into an outside hall that echoes our splashing shoes. It's like one of those old detective movies in a gray fallen down city. This deserted building seems to exist just for this season, a hallway that has exactly one place to go. Dull light sinks into a courtyard. The only color is the bright red painted cement statue of Santa Claus towering in the middle of this empty place. He must be a hundred feet tall. We take our places at the balcony. I grab the railing for a moment but it belongs on a submarine. Winter raindrops spear my hands.

The statue laughs and wishes us, "Merry Christmas!" The voice buzzes and echoes in this landscape. I know it comes from a microphone and I know there's a man hidden inside, pressing buttons and pulling levers like the Wizard of Oz. "What would you like for Christmas?" it booms. My sister leans out as far as she can and I listen as she ticks off her list. You have to believe. Whoever hides inside all that cement could still make it come true. It's happened before.

# TIGER STORY

Brakes hitch and tires skid to the curb. A car door bursts open, rock music, yelling, and the door slams shut. We stop our game on the grassy hill above and stare. Three guys race away from the car, down our sidewalk below us without any clothes. "Streakers!" we both yelp. They whoop and leap off the curb. One of them wears high-top sneakers, and they run in front of a car and hoot again. They laugh and slap feet past the white house on the corner, under the tree, heading for busy 50th Street. Their car lurches from the curb and we can see the girl driving it, holding her hand to her mouth, laughing, following where they went. I can't see if she is naked too. Of course we know about this latest rage, we talk about it on the playground, but we never expected to be this close to it. A truck from the circus could have spilled out tigers on our street. We can tell the story tomorrow at school, but who will believe us?

from the circus

## IN the AIR

On a hot sunny summer day, I sit on the concrete steps. I'm waiting for Jesse's car to arrive. His mom will be wearing her brown waitress uniform. I'll see the checkered sleeve of it as she waves to me. Birds are singing, and I watch a black cat across the street, slow as a shadow on the mowed grass. I hope the birds have the sense to stay in their trees. It reminds me of *Peter and the Wolf.* I can hear my record play the song.

Another song also plays, drifting my way from the top of the tree covered hill. The weather and wind conditions have to be just right. It isn't some report I can tune on my transistor radio. "Traffic's tied up on the Renton S-curves…" a static crackle, "and now here's Susan with the zoo conditions."

I hear a lion. Its roar carries over all the blocks and rooftops. There's a pocket in the air full of lion and I wonder how far it will go. Maybe no further than our climbing tree. Maybe it will settle in those laurel leaves and go to sleep.

A new sound in the air makes me turn

on my cement chair to look for the airplane making that noise round and round. A black dot trails cloudy letters. I don't know how they write in the air, but they do. A lazy wispy M is left on the blue and another letter starts next to it. A crow is cawing. It's probably reading it too, calling other crows nearby. The first word is a girl's name Mary, and the crows and I wait for the plane to move a little more to the right. Another M is done. Just one more letter then the plane drifts from its message and leaves: MARY ME.

these little movies

I was happy to find all these places again. I was grateful the memories were mostly good. Whatever force acted to guide and protect me back then was still working now to reveal all these little movies. They played like dreams I was sometimes in, and sometimes watching. Together they formed a Tin Can Telephone Book. Anytime I wanted, I could pick it up and fall into a memory, just like a random placed call. I want other people to know about it too. I would like there to be Tin Can Telephone Booths for anyone to use. I don't know if these phones would have the same effect for everyone, but it's worth a try. Who knows, maybe it would bring them to other places besides childhood? A girl jumps into a future world. There are unlimited possibilities. A boy suddenly drops into the mind of an elephant, listening to crickets, snapping rope, footsteps, watching through its eyes as it escaped from a circus at night and hid in an overgrown creek bed. You would be taking a chance in the Tin Can Telephone Booth. You might find yourself anywhere.

# FISHING

*Splash!* I am supposed to be stepping from the dock, over the gap of seawater, to get on the boat. I'm thinking of *Jaws* though. That's all anyone can talk about at school and all I can think of this close to the ocean. I see my hovering reflection holding a fishing pole, but I'm sure there's a shark below me. I'm so positive, I lost the use of my arm and I let go.

There was a moment when time froze. The splash makes a flower. It hangs in the air then collapses in on itself and turns to rippling waves as the image of the fishing pole sinks further into the deep green.

It's gone for good.

I still have the bait in my other hand. A bucket full of dead minnows.

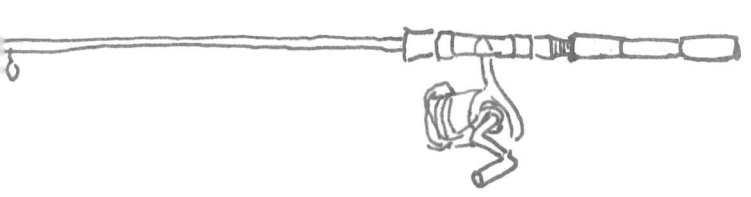

when time froze

# The SUNGLASSES

Channel 5 used to have a show called *How Come?* Through no fault of my own, I ended up on it as well as the local news all on the same night. I've never been able to match such notoriety.

It begins with the hiss of air. My creation breathes in helium and comes to life.

Other kids are spread out on the floor around me with their projects.

A TV camera is filming the class.

"What are you making?"

"A pair of giant sunglasses," I reply.

The taped together plastic garbage bags crackle as it rises off the carpet.

"Sunglasses that fly?" the lady with the microphone asks.

I nod. The black shades lead it into the air, with the limp frame handles dragging like heavy wings. "A little more helium," I say.

Once it is afloat, she reminds me, "Be sure to watch *How Come?* tonight," and I say okay.

On the way to the car though, the glasses get away from me. I let go of the rope by accident. It was pulling like a Great Dane. It shoots across the parking lot and lifts itself gracefully airborne.

I think that's the end and I feel bad until I see it again on TV at home. First it appears on *How Come?* when there are a couple seconds of me making it, saying, "A pair of giant sunglasses." Next we see it LIVE as the story unfolds on the news.

A shaky shot of it hovering over Seattle.

Then the voice in the KIRO-7 Chopper tells us, "We're not exactly sure what we're looking at..."

Back on the set, the anchorman says confidently, "Chuck, I gotta tell you. That looks a lot like a bra."

# The AQUA THEATRE

"Good evening ladies and gentlemen." On the next block up the street from us, the neighborhood has its very own theater. Every block is a continent, I know every sidewalk slab of ours, but this is uncharted territory. Still, I walk past this tall fence every day on the way to school and back. That's how I saw the crayon sign taped to the slats:

THE CASTLE DRAGON
Tonight Only
7 o'clock
Tickets
$1 for adults
50¢ for kids

Once you climb the steep cement stairs and pass through the gate, there's a princess in a dress who puts money into a shoebox. I've never been in this backyard, I don't even know if these kids go to our school. They might go to the church up the street where they wear uniforms and play inside a fence. People are already sitting in the folding chairs, kitchen chairs, on stools and even a couple of couches set on the lawn before the stage. They dragged out everything useful from inside the house. It's okay. It's only temporary. I've played on the remains of The Aqua Theatre half sinking like Atlantis on the shores of Green Lake. Tall floor lamps light the blankets thrown down on the grass and yellowy lanterns are strung overhead. A clothesline reaches from a tree to the garage and a lazy tartan curtain is slung over it to hide the actors and the cardboard castle from view. The director is a thirteen year old boy with a paper crown who holds up the arms of his bathrobe and tells us to quiet down.

"Guess what I have?" Billy Mitchell grins and holds up a crumpled paper bag.

"A tarantula?"

"Wrong." He puts his hand in and takes out something resembling a small mummified lollipop. He waits for us to respond.

"What is it?"

"A stink bomb!" Then he's happy when we crowd around closer. "Guess what I'm going to do with it?"

"Bomb something?"

"I'm going to stink bomb Food Giant!"

We follow him like fools. He explains his plan, how he's going to set it off in the dog food aisle. We stop before going inside and he tells us to be ready to run. Jesse looks nervous. We watch Billy Mitchell follow an old man and turn towards the aisles.

"Hi there!" The manager smiles at me. He's holding a watermelon.

"Hello." Now I feel like an outlaw. He still remembers me from the Robin Hood contest and here I am in a gang about to bomb his store.

But he smiles, "See you around," and turns to carry that watermelon indoors.

Five seconds ticked. We knew it was going to happen. Then it did.

First Billy Mitchell appears around the check-out, running full tilt, followed by the sound of someone screaming. Jesse and I step back from the doorway.

"Run!"

More people inside are reacting. I hear someone coughing and more yelling. Jesse pulls my arm and we run around the brick corner.

Billy Mitchell is half a block from us already. He leaps off the curb and we chase him across the street where we can hide behind the hedges next to the other parking lot. I take a quick look behind us and I don't see the manager or the butcher jumping out the back door.

We collapse on the sidewalk and wait until we can talk.

Billy laughs. "You should have seen it!"

"Did they recognize you?"

"Of course not," Billy grins, "I took off!"

We listen. We're hoping to hear pandemonium spill from Food Giant.

Nothing.

Billy Mitchell gradually peers over the hedge.

He's still holding the crumpled paper bag balled in his hand. I remember the first time I met him, the first day of third grade. He offered me a stick of gum from a pack that snapped like a miniature mousetrap when you pulled one out. "I want to see what's happening." He can't resist. He leaves us and runs back. He's already on the road to doing time and he doesn't know the first rule of his chosen life: you never go back to the scene of the crime.

# The CITY DUMP

This is what it would be like if you were tiny, on a raft in the stomach of a robot. My dad has the sliding door open and is pulling out the black garbage bags. I hop out the van into the noise, onto the oil stained ground, and take one too. It's heavy as a sack of coal. I can't carry two at a time like he can, I have to use both hands and walk like Igor in a foggy cemetery. Not only is the dump loud with crashing, smashing, grumbling engines, breaking glass, the surrounding smell is just as deafening. A foghorn blast of bad air. I try to hold my breath but I only get as far as the edge. Yellow warning lines are painted on the cement and ledge. You don't want to fall off. Seagulls are watching me. A bulldozer pushes piles of broken waves. A refrigerator, a baby carriage, crunching tangles and a dented boiler you could use as a submarine. I wish I could throw the garbage bag way out into it, but it only rolls away from me like a hippo. I hear the splash. In the future, if an archaeologist were to dig ten feet down they would find all this evidence of when we were here. They could piece it together, rebuild a replica like a Roman town from what they found.

What I'm really looking for on this dumped out mountain is a little plywood shack. Somewhere it floats on a moat of tin cans and rust. I've never seen the outside of J.P. Patches' house but that's how I picture it. All I know is he broadcasts his show from his room out here in the trash and invites lucky visitors to his shack. I don't see any sign of it though. It's a good home for Templeton, the rat from *Charlotte's Web*, not J.P. Patches. I try hard to picture kids and field trips and Bluebird troops wandering through these dangers. There has to be a way of getting there from here.

# The 10¢ MUMMY

A dime scratches, pressed into the worn slot and I use both hands to crank the dial. Gears are clicking, the ancient motor inside begins to grind and I can feel the humming vibration through the glass. In a moment, the mummy starts to move in the case, sitting upright as it can manage. That's all it does, but isn't that enough? It's two thousand years old! Then it lies down again, and the motor stops. That's all the money I have. It has all the time in the world, waiting for someone else to come along. The cold basement hallway of the Seattle Center Armory is mostly an echo, a water fountain that leaks on the floor. The mummy knows it can't compete with the Food Court upstairs and the futuristic Bubbleator, but this is the first place I always go.

# TWO DIFFERENT WORLDS

The rope against the flagpole clangs lightly while we make a row like a clothesline. Little did we know we are learning the difference between outside and inside: they're two different worlds. Walking back into our classroom, the smell of chalkboard dust at the front of the room, the silver tray lined with books for reading time, including the one I like, *The Mouse and the Motorcycle*, and as we march under the American flag, we all separate boy, girl, boy, girl, to return to our desks.

We sit down, get quiet and write.

I'm lucky for now: I have a good view, my desk is next to a window. Underneath it, the radiator hisses and taps out a message. It looks like our pencils are trying to decipher that secret code.

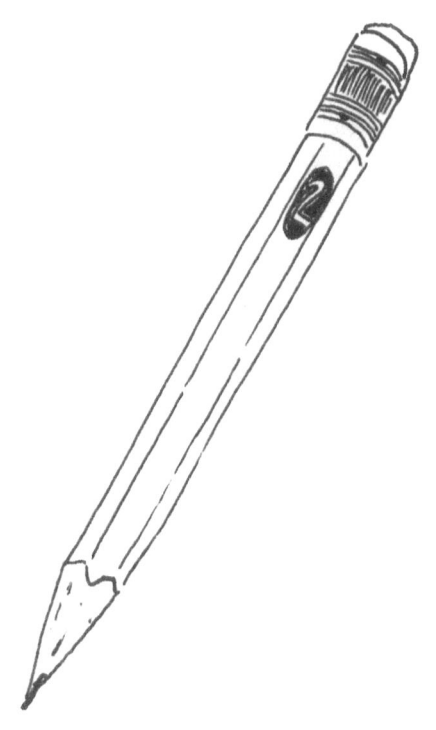

that secret code

# ECOLOGY

Saturday morning, a *Roadrunner* cartoon then *The Ant and the Aardvark* is on. Cartoons are outside too, the sun makes everything bright as one and the city is always churning. I have a chore to do and two blocks to walk to get there.

Down the street at the end of the block I wait for a motorcycle to pass. There goes Runaway Ralph, I think. That's the book I'm reading now. I cross Stone Way after he's gone. When I'm here it feels like I'm on a boat that just passed through the fog. A jungle island appears, with a beach sidewalk going all around. There are P-Patch community gardens all over town, wherever people have dug up the cement.

We share a spot with our neighbors. A path starts between sunflowers tall as Frankenstein, into all the vines, leaves and petals, vegetables, flags and hand-painted signs. A bumblebee tumbles in front of me. The dragonflies and swallows aren't out yet but they will be soon. I tap the wind-chimes on my way. Someone left a robot made of tin cans to rust in the middle of tomatoes. More paths branch off.

With plants getting taller every sunny day, it's starting to turn into a maze. I know where I'm going though.

A spigot emerges from the earth like a periscope. I attach the end of our hose to it, screw it tight then follow the hose into our plot of garden. We have a scarecrow named Stan. I open the nozzle and instant rain hisses. I have to water everything, even Stan. He doesn't seem to mind. He has a long day ahead of him, chasing off crows. All the leaves shine and drip. Tap, tap, tap, the ground turns wet and chocolate colored.

# KRISTINE

Kristine holds the wheel off the ground and gives it a spin. "Just listen to that," she says. It is a silver whisper. Effortlessly, the wheel seems able to turn forever. A perpetual motion machine. Today is Kristine's birthday and this new yellow 10-speed bicycle is hers. I can't believe it. It's like her parents gave her a car, or a bank account. With a ballerina move, she stops the wheel against the toe of her shoe and asks, "You want to go for a ride with me?"

"Sure."

She's wearing a polka dot shirt. Her bright hair shines on her shoulders. Sometime I'd just like to keep looking at her face. I really like those freckles. They're like stars. When her copper painted hair was wet in the rain, she must have shaken off a thousand drops that landed all over her skin. Anytime it's fall and the orange leaves are falling, I think of her.

She's ahead of me—that new bike is quick as a rabbit. I turn right at the corner to follow her and she's already pressing the button to cross 50th. I have to stand on my pedals to get a little speed going. I like to think of my bike as a jet or a spaceship but it can't compete with that girl waiting for me at the crosswalk.

"Come on slowpoke!" she smiles.

The cars are slowing for a red light. On the other side is Woodland Park. I know where I'd go if I had a brand new 10-speed and I wanted to test pilot it. I don't have to ask her as we cross. Sure enough, she hops back on her bike and starts uphill in first gear. I can't go far with her, I think my rocket engine must be in need of repair. I hop off onto the tipped sidewalk so I can push my shot-up starship.

Kristine is a ways ahead. The cars rush by close. Once I had to chase my dog up 50th when she escaped our yard. Looks like Kristine has already made it to the top. I sure could have used a bicycle like that when I had to run after my dog that day.

Kristine waves to me. I wave back. I can't see her after she turns and points her bike towards the soapbox derby track and disappears behind the trees. I pretend I've got to get there quick. It's an emergency. The racetrack is steep. She could hit a hundred miles per hour on that new bike. Another loud motorcycle roars by. That must be Ralph S. Mouse again. He sure gets around.

I'm panting. I hope Kristine is okay. I don't dare ride down the track full speed. If there's an accident, if she skins her knee, I'll tear off my shirt sleeve like Captain Kirk for her to use as a tourniquet.

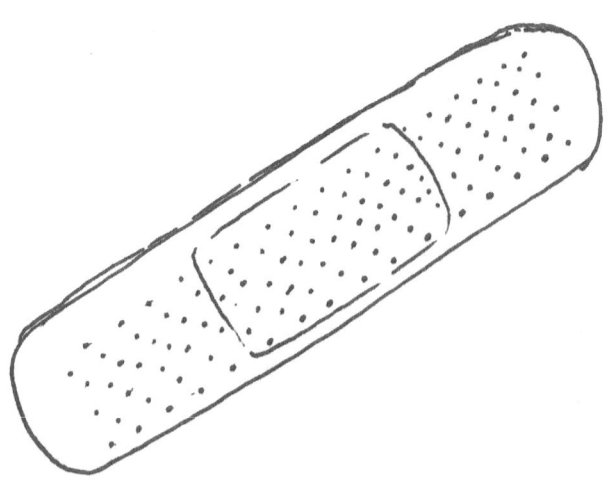

# FIELD TRIP

It isn't a real rain, it's a recording. The class is quiet as we stand in a cold black room. It seems like the museum even fanned in the smell of a wet winter day. A fine silver curtain also gives the illusion of falling rain. The first white settlers are frozen on the beach, looking hopeless. A woman holds a baby covered in a soaked blanket. They're still in the rowboat, they're not ready to step out into thick mudflat. Their leader holds his bleeding arm where he slipped getting out with his axe, slogging his way onto the shore where Chief Seattle is standing. He came out of the woods when he saw their sailing ship round the point and drop anchor. The smoke from the longhouse paints its way through the firs. I hear a wax seagull. The Beatles are waiting for us around the next dark corner.

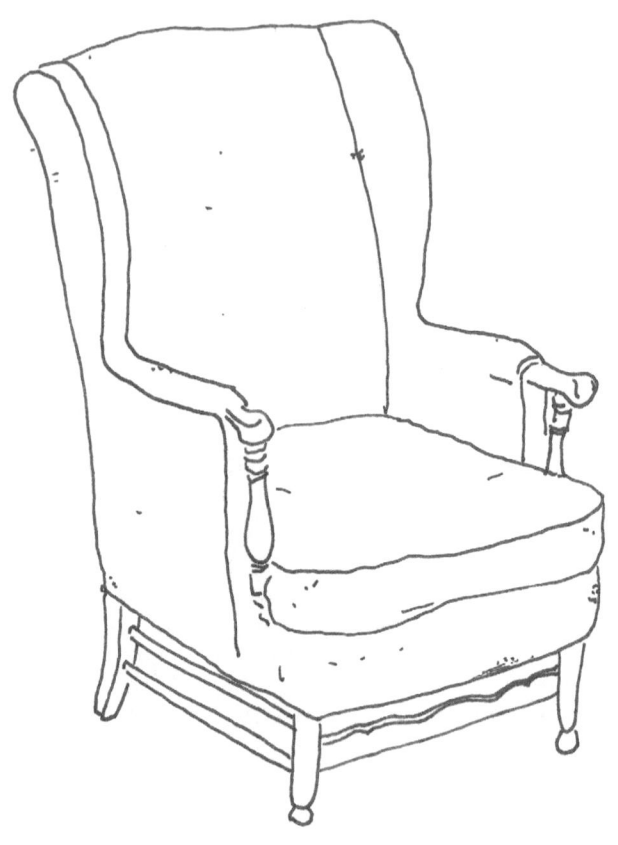

when people pretend

# TACOMA

Thirty miles south on I-5 is the city of Tacoma and the shopping center where we are going to see a gorilla. Am I scared to face another gorilla? As I told Jesse that night at the KJR Haunted House, "Real gorillas are okay, I just don't like when people pretend to be them. Remember what happened to Bob Hope in that movie?"

If I am worried, I'm not showing it. I'm singing along with Otis Redding. The cars are swimming around on either side of us. One time I saw J.P. Patches on the highway, just past the Sunny Jim factory. He pulled up beside us. His car was filled with balloons. He was looking straight ahead, serious, like our dog staring down the highway.

Jesse brought along a bag of licorice and offers it.

"These would make good shoelaces," I say and Jesse agrees.

The gorilla was half an hour away, then fifteen minutes, then five, then we are turning into the parking lot. A big red sign, Saturn Circus Shopping Center in letters that jiggle with neon.

Jesse's mother finds a parking spot. I've never been here before but hop out on the tar like I have. Isn't that what Flash Gordon would do?

We go inside and it smells of popcorn and sawdust. I see a girl with a rainbow lollypop the size of her head. We follow Jesse's mom, she knows the way to Pongo. We pass a player piano making a racket, all the keys going by themselves. There's one of those at Pizza & Pipes too. Seems like a strange invention. I guess they are for when the piano player goes on vacation. Or for The Invisible Man Convention. I told Jesse there should one of those at the Kingdome and he laughed.

Canoes are stacked on the wall, a collection of rifles behind the counter, camouflage in all sizes—it looks like you could plan a safari from here. Jesse's mom points at a plain doorway ahead of us. "There it is."

A frame the size of a window is filled with photos of Pongo. I give it a glance but Jesse and I are ready to see the real thing. The sign above the doorway welcomes us to: PONGO AT HOME. A lady with a big white pocketbook blocks the view in front of us. She says,

"Gracious!" and we have to look around her to see what's going on.

We have stepped before a sort of aquarium wall made of thick glass.

Pongo's room is well lit. There's a chandelier and a tall standing lamp on either side of his couch. He is sitting there peacefully, wearing a bathrobe, holding a newspaper. He has a record player and we can see the Beethoven album spinning next to him. On the coffee table is a white bowl filled with bananas. He also has a typewriter, but we can't read the words typed on the page.

"Look!" Jesse pokes the glass, pointing.

There's also a TV set. It's turned towards Pongo, but we can see part of the screen, enough to know it's *Gilligan's Island*. The only time I watch that is at Jesse's house because he likes it I guess. But I also notice the show is in color. Pongo's got a color TV.

"Look at the painting on the wall," Jesse's mom whispers. "It's a self-portrait."

That's true. Pongo painted himself wearing a blue top hat. Holding an ice cream cone too. Triple scoop!

He's still reading the paper. I bet he does the crosswords too. He crosses his legs and we see the slippers he's wearing. Moccasins, the kind I want.

Jesse's mom leans and asks, "He sure keeps his room tidy, doesn't he Jesse?" with just a hint of a smile. She isn't wearing her brown restaurant uniform today. This is her day off.

I know what she means but Jesse's room seems fine to me. She's got a funny sense of humor though.

Finally Pongo sets *The Seattle Times* down and stands up. I'm ready for him to come pound on the window like *Planet of the Apes* but instead he pads to the kitchen. When I spot what he's after I tell Jesse, "He's got cake!"

We watch him cut a big chocolate piece. When he went to the refrigerator I was expecting him to take out a quart bottle of ice cold milk. We see him reach for the pitcher in there. Jesse cries, "And lemonade!"

Pongo ignores us. Why does he care what we think? He takes his snack back to the couch and sets the plate and tall glass on the plaid cushion beside him.

Leisurely, Pongo turns the page of his newspaper and gives it a lazy shake. What a life!

I wonder if Jesse's mother brought me here on purpose. She was there that night at the

Seattle Center. She knows about that other gorilla I had trouble with. Cowboys always tell each other to get back up and try again when they get thrown. Okay, it worked, I'm not afraid of gorillas. Not this one anyway.

# BELLS & BAGPIPES

It seems like it happens every Sunday morning, but is that true? The bells are ringing in the church tower three blocks from here. I'm lying in bed listening. The clang in the air reminds me of the wind-chimes I made for the climbing tree—they are the same sort of music. I tied them to a branch as far up as I could reach. What happened to them? They were made of tin cans and silverware. A storm must have blown them down. They must have tangled tight together and rolled off the hill in the wind like a hermit crab.

I pull the blanket over my eyes to hide the light and I wait.

The distant church bells come from one direction and then from another I hear something else climb into the air. They hover at the same time, the two have blended and become one sound.

Past Olsen's house there's an old man who stands on the sidewalk and plays the bagpipes. I've only heard the stories about him. I never got out of bed, got dressed and walked over to see him. By the time I got there he would be gone anyway. Olsen said he tried but was too late—there was no sign of him on that sidewalk. As soon as the bells stop so does he.

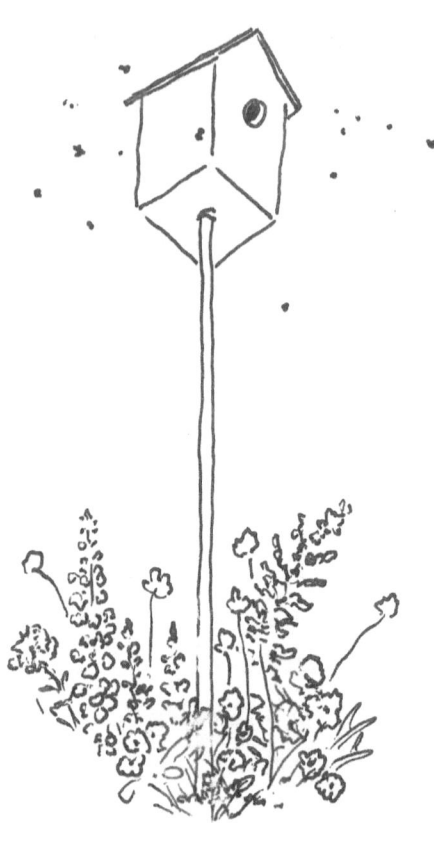

a song in the sky

## The BIRDHOUSE BEES

Bees! They seem to be wherever I go when I'm running on the sidewalk, through the park, digging into the leaves on the streambank— the gardens at the P-Patch spin with them. I've spent a lot of time where they are so I have had my share of getting stung. The sun would be singing a song in the sky and next thing I knew it would happen. One time Billy Mitchell led me into a nest of yellow jackets. Firsthand, I got to know the different species of bees, wasps and hornets. When I want to find out more, I take a walk to the library.

Over Woodlawn, under the telephone wires, onto 46th and right on the next corner, past Food Giant on 45th and Fuji's Five and Dime. We cut across the busy street at the WALK streetlight and follow Meridian Avenue. Houses and yards and trees. Crows on a roof. Someone pushing a lawnmower. A small brick house between two wooden houses always reminds me of the Big Bad Wolf story. There's even barking coming from the backyard. Maybe he's back there?

The library is another house, set on a grassy

front yard, up some cement stairs and a path. A hand-painted sign by the screen door. I open the door and it's as if a magic spell was put on an ordinary house, turning it into a library. Every room is a different subject. Where there was a kitchen, instead of a stove and refrigerator and sink, it's filled with books on world history. The dining room is replaced by fiction. I know just where I'm going though, down a hallway stacked with a million pages into what must have been someone's bedroom. Now it's all children's books. Over where there might have been a bed is where the animals are. I've looked at every dinosaur book many times. I avoid the books on sharks. *The How and Why Wonder Book of Ants and Bees*. I get another one next to it too, *All Kinds of Bees*. They should be enough for now—I'm mindful that I will have to carry them a ways back home. One time I had to carry five airplane books and my arms were stretched long as Pongo's. I bet he has library books delivered though.

On the way home I take Sunnyside Avenue, past more rows of houses. Every block is a different planet. In my imagination I can be on a boat or a plane or someone in a wagon train. I walk beside an overgrown yard full of tall weeds and goldenrod. The house looks like one a family of ghosts would live in.

Wouldn't that be funny if I opened one of my bee books and some of them flew out? That sounds like something that would happen on *Sesame Street*. I can see that happening to Grover.

I smell the next garden before I get there. The flowers reach right out over the sidewalk. A crowd of them fills her yard. It's hard to find a spot where no flowers are growing. Standing up above it like an extra tall flower is a rusted pole with a birdhouse on top. Not for swallows, the occupants are a thousand honey bees. Their beehive is stuffed behind every window and the round doorway. Bees fly around it in a hazy halo and they're all muttering. Some are going in, some are leaving. They follow an invisible path in the air.

a waitress shadow

## The GREAT AMERICAN WHAT

The hall leads to the kitchen. I always run my hand along the red wallpaper that feels like fur. I like to stop at the window and watch the circus. The Great American What is one of my favorite restaurants. You'll see why. The cook tosses a ball of fire in his frying pan. He's wearing vampire teeth and a cape. Behind him is a mime. The mime holds her hand in front of her eyes as if blinded as she copies everything he does. I laugh at that. She is a funny shadow of him. When the waitress comes to collect the plate of food, the mime becomes a waitress shadow and follows her out the swinging doors.

Everyone who works here is dressed in costume. The dishwasher is a frogman.

I know my dinner is probably waiting so I don't want to take too long.

First I have to make room for the Statue of Liberty. She is holding a stack of menus against her side. Her other arm isn't up raising the torch. It hangs at her hip. I don't blame her though, that would get awful tiring. Her green face gives me a smile as she passes.

In the middle of the room, a waiter starts

singing. I recognize the cheesy lyrics, it's one of those teenager radio songs Jesse's sister loves. With him singing it, it becomes a comedy. Everyone is turned to watch, some people are even joining in.

I walk past Evel Knievel. He's leaning against one of the posts. I wonder if he'll be jumping over ten tables later. I don't have time to ask him. I can't believe what happens next.

Flash Gordon is heading my way.

He looks the same as when we saw him in the park and at the movie theater, only now he's ten feet from me and closing. There's no time to move or find the words.

"How are you?" he asks.

I must be star-struck. This is what it's like.

"You look like a smart kid," he tells me and I still can't say a thing. I wish I could. I wish I could tell him how much I like seeing him and Dale Arden running through another world. "Can I give you some advice?"

I do manage to nod. At least I can do that.

"Make sure you eat your broccoli," he tells me. He's been holding a tray of broccoli all this time and he offers one to me.

I forget about trying to speak. I take one and nod again and he pats my shoulder on his path to the kitchen.

I feel like our meeting has made me become a Space Ranger. The broccoli fits in my hand like a mysterious lifeform I'm transporting. I go through a cloud of blue cigarette smoke to a dark window and stare out. I expect to see his rocket ship, sparking and smoking, slant up across the skyline. Over the glow of The Royal Fork, the Guild neon marquee and the Herfy's parking lot, barely avoiding the distant red blinking nose of the Wheedle on the Needle. Maybe I just missed him. All I see in the sky are some stars. On the other side of the street used cars are for sale. Three big spotlights whirl, pointed at outer space. I can see those same lights when I look out my parents' window. Past the lime aura of the baseball field, the car lot lights spin on the north end of Green Lake. On a warm summer night I wish I could sit outside on the steep roof like Otis Redding in his song.

# FAIRPLAY STORAGE

A couple blocks from 7-11 is our destination. Kristine and I go this way sometimes, after school, before our dinners take us home. This might be summer though. She's wearing a yellow dress that almost matches her 10-speed's color. As we roll over the smooth tar surrounding the Post Office, I take my feet off the pedals and coast. "What if you could fly like this?" I ask her.

The wind moves her dress like a sail when she holds her feet off the pedals too. If we could fly, we would go right over the line of telephone wires like two pigeons and land on the gravel lot across the street.

Fairplay Storage is three long buildings placed in a line like army barracks. Our bicycle wheels crackle into the small stones not much bigger than jelly beans. One of these days Kristine says we'll go right up to Building 3. Today we stare at it from the gateway. The blackberries are backed against it as if trying to cover it up. There's a story about what's hiding inside Building 3. Who knows if it's true? I don't see any windows. There's a door, but it's padlocked. If we listened to the metal wall we might hear something.

"Want to go spin the wheel?" Kristine says after a minute.

"Sure."

That's our next stop on our way home, another block from here. Ever since her birthday, Kristine rides her 10-speed to school instead of walking with me and the neighbor girls. My bicycle feels like a Model T compared to what she's riding. She's gone around Green Lake in record time.

I rattle off the curb after her. This building is loud. A big sliding door is open to the parking lot, the printing presses are thudding.

We enter the driveway and leave our bikes beside the loading dock. As we climb onto that platform, one of the workers inside greets us with a wave.

"Hey guys!"

They make the junk mail, advertisements and coupon pages that get stuffed into mailboxes or newspapers. Last time we were here they let us peek at the factory floor. They were printing a neat stapled coupon book for Food Giant. I told Kristine I wanted to make my own book like that and publish it here.

"What's new?" the factory worker asks us.

Kristine shrugs, "Not much."

"I bet you guys want to spin the wheel?" he smiles.

I don't know how Kristine found out about this place. Somehow she did one day when she looked in the loading dock door to find out the warehouse workers made a cardboard roulette wheel-of-fortune. It leans on a low counter by a stack of packing boxes. They let us spin the arrow whenever we stop by. All kinds of funny prizes are written around the circle. My favorite one is Lungfish. What if I actually won a lungfish? I would keep it in a pan of water and it could walk around my room when it wanted to.

"Did you see Building 3?" he asks us on our way to the wheel. Funny we never asked his name. We just show up here, spin and leave.

"It's still there," I say.

"No sign of the UFO?"

"No," I say, "It's still stored in there, I guess."

"Well, one of these days that thing is going to blast right out through the roof of Building #3. Give 'er a spin."

I say, "You can spin first, Kristine."

She does and the arrow goes click, click,

click and what do you know?
   "Lungfish!" we all sing together.

# PENNY CANDY

I shake the piggy bank until every last coin drops out of it onto the green carpet of my room. Jesse is already counting it, but it doesn't take him long.

"49¢," he reports.

Not much, but we're only buying penny candy. Enough to start the engines of the rocket ship we made out of cardboard boxes. It takes up most of my floor. "Okay, let's get going."

Jesse passes me the change and I drop it into my pocket. We cut pieces of tin foil off the roll in the kitchen to make our uniforms. I have a bright silver sun taped to my shirt. Jesse has a moon. We are two stranded Space Rangers. We need to find fuel for the rocket or all is lost.

As we walk along, I warn Jesse about the Planet Mongo. This is a dangerous path, full of monsters—there are Hawkmen, constrictor plants, giant lobsters, poisonous dragons and prowling sabertooths. Not to mention The Merciless Ming. We have to be careful. I point out the flowers that are ready to spring at us. The old lady who lives there put a chain-link fence all around her garden because we used to cross her yard. Either on bicycles or running. Once it was a Big Wheel. Since then, I pretend she lives in a haunted castle and the flowers have to be kept in a cage.

The sidewalk has changed too. I show Jesse how we can only jump on the tree leaf shadows. 48th Street is nowhere to be seen anymore.

We have to wait for two spaceships to pass before we can cross Stone Way which has become a river running through the stars. Three hot suns shine on the jungle ahead of us. We walk along beside the bristling vines and flowers. Dinosaurs howl in there.

"You still have the 49 cents?" Jesse asks.

That's what someone always says in TV shows like this. As if this is the ransom for the return of a princess. Usually it's more than 49¢.

I nod. I can also see the 7-11 store now. "We're almost there," I tell him. "They'll be watching for us." We cross 47th Street, past the ruins of crashed rockets and 7-11 is dead ahead.

I look at the window and see our reflection as one of the chapters in *Rocket Man*.

"Hold on," says Jesse. He's having trouble with the foil moon on his shirt—the tape isn't holding right. He presses the corners as good as he can. "It's okay."

I open the door and we walk into that radio song about being on top of the world. I like to turn the metal stand full of comics to see what they have. I almost stop to check out the *Richie Rich* cover with the robot, but we're on our way to the shelf full of penny candy. There are a lot of different kinds: butterscotch, root beer barrels, taffies, tootsie rolls, Bazooka Joe. Jesse points at what we need. A display box of bright red Atomic Fireballs. Each candy is packaged in its own protective clear wrapper. You can't even touch one by accident without getting burned.

I ask the checker, "Can we count how many Atomic Fireballs are in this box?"

"Sure kid." He looks like a high schooler. He's got a moustache.

I set the cardboard box on the counter and Jesse and I start to take them out.

"What are you guys?"

I don't want to lose count. I say, "eight, nine, ten, eleven…We're from outer space. We need these to start our rocket." Then I pick out the next Atomic Fireball, "Twelve, thirteen," and kept counting until 23.

Jesse says, "I've got 25."

I did the math, adding them together. "That's 48? I wish I could write it down to make sure."

"It's 48," the checker nods. "I took algebra." He thinks that's pretty funny. "How many do you want to buy?"

"I have forty nine cents," I tell him. "We need them all."

"Okay then." He watches us try to scoop all those candies into our cupped hands. "You can keep the box if you want. You can put the candy back in there."

We both say, "Thanks!" in stereo. I like the bright red and yellow box. I get the money and the checker rings it up. I still have one lucky penny left.

"Outer space?" he asks.

Jesse says, "Yes sir."

"Well, there should be enough of those to get you back." He sorts the silver and copper into the cash drawer and says, "Safe travels," saluting us as we leave.

It feels like Halloween again, dressed in our uniforms, carrying this much candy through my neighborhood. When we get home we can use gloves to drop them one by one into the rocket.

# DRAWN with CHALK

As soon as I put the Tin Can Telephone to my ear, I hear the voices of kids playing. It sounds like recess at some school somewhere. Maybe it's mine, maybe not, I don't see myself in the crowd. They call and sing just like birds on a sunny day. A blue crayon sky, a few white clouds wooly and slow as sheep, trees thick with green leaves. The picture breaks up when it goes quiet. I give the can a shake and put it back to my ear.

For a moment I hear my name. Someone is calling for me. It might be Olsen or Jesse or Kristine. It might be Jack Benny. It might be one of my family or any old voice on the sidewalk, I don't know, it's hard to tell. My name sounds like it's drawn with chalk and then it fades the same way.

I hear a distant jet in the background, the sound of a running faucet being turned off, and that's it.

When I shook the can again, nothing spilled out.

The next time I listened to the Tin Can Telephone nothing happened. I wasn't drawn to another time and place. There was no answer. Just that dull seashell hush. The cans were empty.

To be honest, it wasn't surprising. How many memories could fit in those tin cans before they ran out? It was all magic from the beginning, why did I think it was limitless? There had to be an end.

That was hard to accept though.

Maybe it was only a loose connection. I hoped so. I wondered if someone in town could fix them.

It isn't something you can find in the telephone book, under Tin Can Telephone Repair.

I might be the only one in America with this problem.

The only place I could think to go was the Radio Museum on Railroad Avenue.

# TIN CANS & STRING

It was only a twenty minute bus ride. I carried the Tin Can Telephone in a paper bag. I watched out the window. There are plenty of wires strung along Holly Street. They make the city seem like a marionette. I wondered if all those lines were working right, do they ever wear out? Maybe all my telephone needed was a new string. I should have tried that before I left home.

I got out at the station on Magnolia and it wasn't far to the museum.

I was thinking about the miracle I carried, about all those memory movies and all the time traveling I had done to places I forgot about. There must be hundreds more floating like radio signals beyond the atmosphere, waiting for me.

The red light on Railroad Ave gave me time to wonder about that. Why was the Tin Can Telephone able to magically gather in those transmissions that happened long ago?

In between a row of stores beaded together, cafés and bakeries, a chocolate maker, a shoe repair, a guitar shop and second-hand clothes, the museum is wedged in like a radio tube.

After entering, you realize the room is not much wider than the door, you can almost reach out and touch the walls on either side. Not that you can see wallpaper or any sign of wall, radios are stacked from the floor to the ceiling. Think of the sound if they were all turned on.

A few times I had to turn sideways around floor model cabinets and a jukebox as I made my way to the back of the museum.

"Hello," a man called me from there. He wore a jewelers magnifying lens locked to one eye.

"Are you the radio doctor?" I asked.

He laughed. He held up the one he was working on. "My current patient."

"Do you know about telephones?" They seem similar to radios, don't they both broadcast? "Mine stopped working, I was hoping you could take a look." I showed him the paper bag. "I brought it along."

"You can leave it on the table here. I'm in the middle of another repair at the moment."

"Of course. Thanks so much for your help." I set the crumpled grocery bag next to a broken car radio. He had plenty more to get to, waiting on the table to work again.

A bright circle shined like a spotlight where his hands performed. They were magnified by his eyepiece so he could see far into radio worlds. I started to leave but he reached out of the full moonlight and I heard him pick up that crackly bag.

First he looked inside and then he looked at me. Then he looked into the bag again and said, "Are you kidding me?"

"No."

"This is your telephone?"

"Yes."

He dug into the bag and pulled out one can strung to another. He laughed as they spun a little, like a toy. He was going to say something, until he realized I really believed he could help. So he got serious and began again, "Well, let me see..." He examined each can carefully, picking off a few spots where the old label was stuck on. No dents or mars. A minor scratch. He tested the string. He rolled it between two fingers checking for unraveling. He gave each can a tap, close to his ear. When he listened to them though, I could tell he wasn't transported. Finally he told me, "I've looked them over for you and I examined them every possible way...

You know what? They're just tin cans and string."

The TIN CAN TELEPHONE
Written June—October 2019

Page from *Roosevelt* (2015)
Illustrated by Fred Sodt

# Books by Good Deed Rain

*Saint Lemonade*, Allen Frost, 2014. Two novels illustrated by the author in the manner of the old Big Little Books.

*Playground*, Allen Frost, 2014. Poems collected from seven years of chapbooks.

*Roosevelt*, Allen Frost, 2015. A Pacific Northwest novel set in July, 1942, when a boy and a girl search for a missing elephant. Illustrated throughout by Fred Sodt.

*5 Novels*, Allen Frost, 2015. Novels written over five years, featuring circus giants, clockwork animals, detectives and time travelers.

*The Sylvan Moore Show*, Allen Frost, 2015. A short story omnibus of 193 stories written over 30 years.

*Town in a Cloud*, Allen Frost, 2015. A three part book of poetry, written during the Bellingham rainy seasons of fall, winter, and spring.

*A Flutter of Birds Passing Through Heaven: A Tribute to Robert Sund*. 2016. Edited by Allen Frost and Paul Piper. The story of a legendary Ish River poet & artist.

*At the Edge of America*, Allen Frost, 2016. Two novels in one book blend time travel in a mythical poetic America.

*Lake Erie Submarine*, Allen Frost, 2016. A two week vacation in Ohio inspired these poems, illustrated by the author.

*and Light*, Paul Piper, 2016. Poetry written over three years. Illustrated with watercolors by Penny Piper.

*The Book of Ticks*, Allen Frost, 2017. A giant collection of 8 mysterious adventures featuring Phil Ticks. Illustrated throughout by Aaron Gunderson.

*I Can Only Imagine*, Allen Frost, 2017. Five adventures of love and heartbreak dreamed in an imaginary world. Cover & color illustrations by Annabelle Barrett.

*The Orphanage of Abandoned Teenagers*, Allen Frost, 2017. A fictional guide for teens and their parents. Illustrated by the author.

*In the Valley of Mystic Light: An Oral History of the Skagit Valley Arts Scene*, 2017. Edited by Claire Swedberg & Rita Hupy.

*Different Planet*, Allen Frost, 2017. Four science fiction adventures: reincarnation, robots, talking animals, outer space and clones. Cover & illustrations by Laura Vasyutynska.

*Go with the Flow: A Tribute to Clyde Sanborn*. 2018. Edited by Allen Frost. The life and art of a timeless river poet.

*Homeless Sutra*, Allen Frost, 2018. Four stories: Sylvan Moore, a flying monk, a water salesman, and a guardian rabbit.

*The Lake Walker*, Allen Frost 2018. A little novel set in black and white like one of those old European movies about death and life.

*A Hundred Dreams Ago*, Allen Frost, 2018. A winter book of poetry and prose. Illustrated by Aaron Gunderson.

*Almost Animals*, Allen Frost, 2018. A collection of linked stories, thinking about what makes us animals.

*The Robotic Age*, Allen Frost, 2018. A vaudeville magician and his faithful robot track down ghosts. Illustrated throughout by Aaron Gunderson.

*Kennedy*, Allen Frost, 2018. This sequel to *Roosevelt* is a coming-of-age fable set during two weeks in 1962 in a mythical Kennedy-land. Illustrated throughout by Fred Sodt.

*Fable*, Allen Frost, 2018. There's something going on in this country and I can best relate it in fable: the parable of the rabbits, a bedtime story, and the diary of our trip to Ohio.

*Elbows & Knees: Essays & Plays*, Allen Frost, 2018. A thrilling collection of writing about some of my favorite subjects, from B-movies to Brautigan.

*The Last Paper Stars*, Allen Frost 2019. A trip back in time to the 20 year old mind of Frankenstein, and two other worlds of the future.

*Walt Amherst is Awake*, Allen Frost, 2019. The dreamlife of an office worker. Illustrated throughout by Aaron Gunderson.

*When You Smile You Let in Light*, Allen Frost, 2019. An atomic love story written by a 23 year old.

*Pinocchio in America*, Allen Frost, 2019. After 82 years buried underground, Pinocchio returns to life behind a car repair shop in America.

*Taking Her Sides on Immortality*, Robert Huff, 2019. The long awaited poetry collection from a local, nationally renowned master of words.

*Florida*, Allen Frost, 2019. Three days in Florida turned into a book of sunshine inspired stories.

*Blue Anthem Wailing*, Allen Frost, 2019. My first novel written in college is an apocalyptic, Old Testament race through American shadows while Amelia Earhart flies overhead.

*The Welfare Office*, Allen Frost, 2019. The animals go in and out of the office, leaving these stories as footprints.

*Island Air*, Allen Frost, 2019. A detective novel featuring haiku, a lost library book and streetsongs.

*Imaginary Someone*, Allen Frost, 2020. A fictional memoir featuring 45 years of inspirations and obstacles in the life of a writer.

*Violet of the Silent Movies*, Allen Frost, 2020. A collection of starry-eyed short story poems, illustrated by the author.

*The Tin Can Telephone*, Allen Frost, 2020. A childhood memory novel set in 1975 Seattle, illustrated like a coloring book.

JANUARY 19

Sunday

19 I played with Kristine, I watched a movie about a Monster it was neat. I watched a show called How Come?

19

19

from the author's 1975 diary